P9-CRZ-424

Walt Disney's

Winnie the Pooh and the Honey Tree

Janet Campbell

Illustrated by John Kurtz

New York

Printed and bound in the United States of America.
For information address Disney Press,
114 Fifth Avenue, New York, New York 10011.

9 10 8

Library of Congress Catalog Card Number: 92-53442
ISBN: 1-56282-379-5

Walt Disney's

Winnie the Pooh and the Honey Tree

One sunny morning, in a little house somewhere deep in the Hundred-Acre Wood, a very round bear named Winnie the Pooh was touching his toes. He was breathing deeply when, all of a sudden, he felt his tummy rumble.

"Oh my," said Pooh. "This exercising is making me hungry."

Pooh hurried to the cupboard and got out his honeypot, but he had already eaten all the honey for breakfast.

"Bother!" said Pooh. "There's nothing left but the sticky part."

But since the sticky part was better than *no* honey at all, Pooh stuck his nose into the pot as far as it would go and licked up the last little patches left at the bottom.

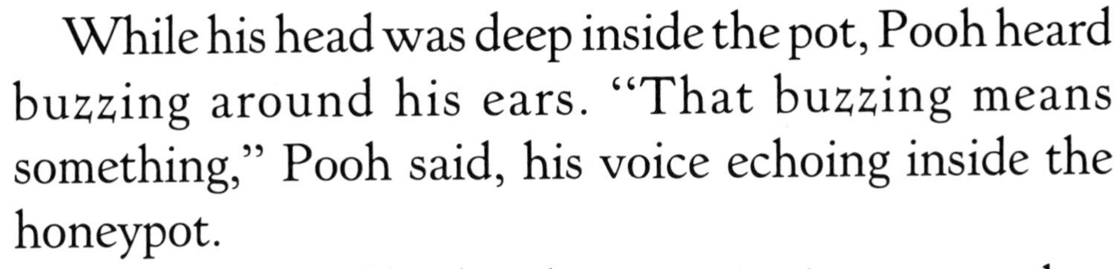

While his head was deep inside the pot, Pooh heard buzzing around his ears. "That buzzing means something," Pooh said, his voice echoing inside the honeypot.

Pop! He pulled his head out just in time to see a bee fly out his window.

"Oh!" said Pooh. "A bee! And where there are bees, there is usually honey!"

Pooh followed the bee through the Hundred-Acre Wood until he came to the foot of a very tall tree. When he looked up, he saw the bee buzzing around a hole in the tree.

"Honey!" said Pooh, and he began to climb. He climbed and he climbed, all the way up the tree, until he reached a branch right next to the hole.

As Pooh leaned toward the hole, the branch began to bend. The more he leaned, the more the branch bent, until he could almost reach the honey.

Then he leaned just a little bit more...and *snap!* went the branch and down went Pooh...

...bouncing from branch to branch to branch

until he ran out of branches...

…and landed headfirst in a bush!

"Oh my," said Pooh, rubbing his sore head. "I guess it all comes from liking honey so much!"

Pooh rubbed his head so hard that he came up with an idea.

First, he borrowed a balloon from his friend Christopher Robin. "But you can't get honey with a balloon," Christopher Robin told Pooh.

"*I* can," said Pooh. "I shall hang on to the string and float up to the bee hole," he explained.

Then Pooh rolled himself in mud until he was covered from his nose to his toes.

"I'm pretending to be a little black storm cloud," Pooh told Christopher Robin, "to fool the bees."

"Silly old bear," said Christopher Robin as he watched Pooh float up, up, up into the sky and dangle right outside the hole.

Pooh reached in and pulled out a pawful of golden honey. But the bees began to buzz suspiciously around his head.

"Christopher Robin!" called Pooh, swatting at the bees and swinging wildly from the end of the balloon string. "I think the bees suspect that I am not a little black storm cloud!"

All of a sudden the balloon's string loosened, and the balloon began to lose air. It swooshed under Pooh and it swooshed over Pooh, and then it rose high above the treetops, with Pooh trailing along for the ride.

"Oh my," said Pooh, taking in the sights.

Then the balloon had no more air at all, and down Pooh went, landing right on top of Christopher Robin!

"Oh dear," said Pooh, shaking his head. "I guess it all comes from liking honey so much!"

By then it was lunchtime, and Pooh was hungrier than ever. So he sat down to think, and he thought first about honey and then about Rabbit, because Rabbit always had some honey in his house.

Pooh hurried to Rabbit's house and invited himself in.

"Uh...er...come in, Pooh," said Rabbit.

"Why, thank you, Rabbit," said Pooh.

"How about some lunch?" Rabbit asked, knowing perfectly well what Pooh's answer would be. "Would you like condensed milk or honey on your bread?"

"Both," Pooh answered politely. "But never mind the bread," he added.

Rabbit sat at the table and watched Pooh eat.
First, Pooh had a little helping of condensed milk and then a little helping of honey. Then he had another helping of condensed milk and another helping of honey. Pooh ate and ate and ate and ate.
MIL

At last, Pooh rose slowly from the table and said in a rather sticky voice, "Good-bye, Rabbit, I must be going."

Rabbit sighed. "Well, Pooh, if you're sure you won't have any more..."

"*Is* there any more?" asked Pooh, sure that he could manage a few more bites.

"No," said Rabbit wearily, "there isn't."

"I thought not," said Pooh, and he started out Rabbit's front door.

But just when Pooh's head had reached the outdoors and his feet were still dangling indoors, his middle got stuck in the middle! Pooh tried to go out. He tried to go in. But he could do neither.

"Bother!" said Pooh. "It all comes from not having a big enough front door."

"Nonsense!" said Rabbit sharply. "It all comes from eating too much!" And off he went, hurrying out his back door to fetch Christopher Robin.

Now there was nothing for Pooh to do but wait. He looked at the trees blowing in the breeze. He watched the clouds sailing by in the blue sky. Then he wiggled his bottom and kicked his legs—just in case—but he was still stuck tight.

So he looked at the trees some more and spotted Owl sitting on a branch.

"Hello, Pooh," said Owl. "Fancy meeting you half in and half out of Rabbit's house. Are you stuck?"

"Oh, no!" said Pooh. "I'm just resting."

Owl swooped down from his branch and looked Pooh square in the eye. "Pooh," he said, "you are definitely stuck. You are a wedged bear in a great tightness. This situation calls for an expert!"

"Did someone say 'expert'?" asked a gopher who just happened to pop out of the ground at that very moment. "Gopher's my name, digging's my game. Now, what seems to be the problem?"

He quickly inspected the situation. "The problem with this door," Gopher said, "is that it has a bear in it. Now we could dig him out, or we could dynamite him out."

"Dynamite?" Pooh said in a very small voice.

"Dynamite!" exclaimed Owl. "Nonsense! We can't dynamite. We might hurt him!"

"Well, think it over," said Gopher, popping back down into his hole. "Let me know if you change your mind."

Finally Rabbit returned with Christopher Robin close behind.

"Silly old bear," said Christopher Robin, shaking his head. Then he took hold of Pooh's paw, and Rabbit took hold of Christopher Robin's shirt, and they pulled and pulled and pulled.

But Pooh was still stuck tight.

"Pooh Bear," said Christopher Robin, "there is only one thing to do. We will have to wait for you to get thin enough to slide out Rabbit's front door!"

So they all waited.

Christopher Robin read stories to Pooh.

Owl lectured him on the dangers of eating too much.

Kanga brought Pooh a kerchief to protect his head from the sun.

Eeyore made gloomy predictions about how long it might take for Pooh to get thinner. "It could be days," he said with a sigh. "Maybe weeks, even months," he added, shaking his head.

After some time had passed, Rabbit grew tired of seeing Pooh's bottom and legs where his front door used to be. He decided to turn Pooh into something better to look at.

First, Rabbit wedged a picture frame around Pooh and put a lace doily on Pooh's bottom. "And now for a little dash of color," he said, setting a flowerpot on top of the doily on top of Pooh.

Next, Rabbit found two branches that looked like antlers and poked them into the frame. Then, with a paintbrush, he began to paint a moose face right on Pooh's bottom. But the paintbrush tickled, and Pooh began to wiggle, which turned Rabbit's moose mouth into a squiggly line.

For a finishing touch, Rabbit found a board and put it across Pooh's legs like a shelf. "Now that's more like it!" he said, arranging some knickknacks on his new shelf.

More time passed, and still the friends waited for Pooh to get thinner.

One afternoon, Kanga brought Roo for a visit. "I brought you a present, Pooh," said Roo. "It's honeysuckle."

"*Honey*suckle?" asked Pooh hungrily. He licked his lips and eyed the bouquet of flowers.

"No, Pooh," said Kanga, laughing. "You don't eat it—you smell it."

Pooh buried his nose in the flowers and sniffed.

"Mmmmm," he said. He sniffed again. "Ahhhh." Then his nose began to tickle. "Ahhhhh," he said once more. "Ah, ah, ah...

"...CHOO!"

Inside Rabbit's hole, Pooh kicked his legs, and down came Rabbit's new shelf, knickknacks and all.

"Oh dear! Oh dear!" said Rabbit crossly. "Why did I ever invite that bear to lunch?"

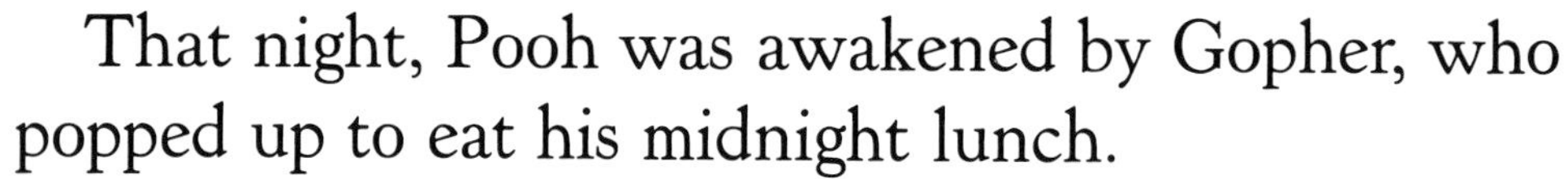

That night, Pooh was awakened by Gopher, who popped up to eat his midnight lunch.

Pooh watched hungrily as Gopher ate. When Gopher took a honeypot from his lunch box, Pooh just couldn't stand it any longer. "Please, Gopher," he pleaded, "could you spare a small smackeral of honey?"

Inside, Rabbit heard voices. Why, he was sure he had just heard someone give Pooh some honey—honey that would make him fatter and keep him stuck in Rabbit's front door even longer.

RABBiTz
HOWSE

"Stop, stop, stop!" Rabbit cried, and he rushed out his back door and around to the front just in time to snatch a honeypot from Pooh's paws. "Not a bite!" he snapped. "Not a lick! Not a drop!" Then he made a sign and stuck it right up in front of Pooh where everyone could see it. It read:

DON'T FEED THE BEAR.

The next morning, Rabbit was busy tidying up. He mopped his brow and leaned against Pooh's bottom to rest.

And Pooh moved!

Rabbit cried out with delight, "He budged! Hooray! He budged!" Rabbit was so excited, he jumped up and down and ran in circles and sang, "He bidged! He badged! He boodged!"

He stopped to catch his breath. "Christopher Robin!" he said. "I must get Crostopher Raban!"

And out his back door Rabbit went, off through the Hundred-Acre Wood, just as fast as he could go.

RABBiTS
HOWSE

Before Pooh even knew what was happening, along came a parade of his very good friends.

Rabbit ran into his house and began to push Pooh's bottom. Christopher Robin ran to the door, grabbed Pooh's paws, and began to pull. Kanga grabbed Christopher Robin, Eeyore grabbed Kanga, Roo grabbed Eeyore, and they all pulled as hard as they possibly could.

Just when they were beginning to think that perhaps Pooh hadn't budged after all, Rabbit backed up in his living room as far as he could go and ran across the floor as fast as he could run and threw himself at Pooh's bottom as hard as he could throw himself.

Pop!

Pooh flew out the doorway like a cork from a bottle and sailed across the grassy place in front of Rabbit's house—straight toward another honey tree. He landed headfirst right inside the hole in the tree.

Buzzzzz! Pooh's sudden appearance startled the bees, and they flew out of the tree and far away over the treetops.

Winnie the Pooh considered his new surroundings. Everywhere he looked, he saw delicious, delightful, mouth-watering honey.

"Don't worry, Pooh!" called Christopher Robin from way down below. "We'll get you out!"

“Take your time, Christopher Robin,” said Pooh. “Take your time!”